SCOOBY-DOO!
An Early Reading Adventure
LOST AT SEA

By Michelle H. Nagler
Illustrated by Duendes del Sur

ABDOPUBLISHING.COM

Reinforced library bound edition published in 2017 by Spotlight, a division of ABDO. PO Box 398166, Minneapolis, Minnesota 55439. Spotlight produces high-quality reinforced library bound editions for schools and libraries. Published by agreement with Warner Bros. Entertainment Inc.

Printed in the United States of America, North Mankato, Minnesota.
042016   092016

THIS BOOK CONTAINS
RECYCLED MATERIALS

PUBLISHER'S CATALOGING IN PUBLICATION DATA

Names: Nagler, Michelle H., author. | Duendes del Sur, illustrator.
Title: Scooby-Doo in lost at sea / by Michelle H. Nagler ; illustrated by Duendes del Sur.
Description: Minneapolis, MN : Spotlight, [2017] | Series: Scooby-Doo early reading adventures
Summary: Scooby and the gang enter a surfboarding contest. But the tides turn when Scooby and Shaggy's board steers them into a deserted part of the beach. Can they make it safely back to their friends?
Identifiers: LCCN 2016930657 | ISBN 9781614794769 (lib. bdg.)
Subjects: LCSH: Scooby-Doo (Fictitious character)--Juvenile fiction. | Dogs--Juvenile fiction. | Contests--Juvenile fiction. | Beaches--Juvenile fiction. | Surfing--Juvenile fiction. | Mystery and detective stories--Juvenile fiction. | Adventure and adventurers--Juvenile fiction.
Classification: DDC [Fic]--dc23
LC record available at http://lccn.loc.gov/2016930657

Spotlight
A Division of ABDO
abdopublishing.com

Scooby and the gang could
hardly wait to get to the beach.
Today they were entering a
surfing contest!
Shaggy had his eye on the
tallest trophy.
"Wouldn't it be cool to win,
Scoob?" Shaggy asked.
"First prize! Scooby-Dooby-Doo!"
agreed Scooby.
The gang heard the whistle.
The contest was about to start.

Velma went first. She stood up on her board and rode a wave all the way to shore.

"Nice ride!" said Steve the lifeguard.

Next to go were Fred and Daphne. They did tricks on their surfboards.

"Nice surfin'," said the lifeguard.

Scooby and Shaggy were up next.

Scooby and Shaggy hopped
on one board and paddled out
from shore.

"Here's our wave," said Shaggy.
"Get ready, Scoob!"

Scooby and Shaggy stood up on
their board. The wave kept
getting bigger and bigger.

They were scared and had no
idea of where they were headed.

Finally, the surfboard hit a rock
and sent them flying onto a big
pile of sand.

"That wave took us way out to sea," said Shaggy. "This must be an island."

"Rare re rost?" asked Scooby.

"Yeah, we are lost," said Shaggy. "Like, Fred, Daphne and Velma will think a sea monster got us! We have to find our way back," Shaggy said.

Scooby and Shaggy looked around for anything that might get them back to the lifeguard station. Scooby found a can, some shells and a friendly crab, but no way off the island.

Then they found a bottle with paper and a pen inside.

"I've got an idea," said Shaggy.

"Scooby-Snack?" asked Scooby.

"Like, time to get off the island!" replied Shaggy.

"We can put a message in this bottle," Shaggy said, holding up the pen.

"Rave us!" said Scooby.

Shaggy wrote SAVE US on the paper and put it in the bottle. Scooby and his new friend the crab tossed the bottle into the sea.

"Someone will find the message and rescue us," said Shaggy.

Shaggy had another idea.
"Maybe we can use the
surfboard to get back to the
beach!" he said.

"Ro ray," Scooby said as he
shook his head and pointed at
the sea. "Rarks!"

Soon, Scooby and Shaggy got hungry. Scooby brought over the can of food he had found.

"Hot dogs! Good job, Scoob!" said Shaggy.

They built a fire and cooked lunch. Suddenly, they heard a noise.

"Something is coming," said Shaggy.

Just then, Fred, Daphne and Velma appeared.

"Did you get our message in the bottle?" asked Shaggy.

"No, we saw the smoke from your fire," said Fred.

"How did you get to our island?" asked Shaggy. "By boat?"

"This is not an island," said Velma. "This is the other end of the beach—past the big rocks."

"Let's surf back!" said Fred.

Scooby shook his head.

"Scoob's afraid of the sharks," said Shaggy.

"Those are dolphins," said Velma. "They won't hurt us."

The gang all climbed on the surfboard and waited for a big wave. They rode the wave all the way back to the beach.

The lifeguard blew his whistle.

"Oh no," said Daphne. "What's wrong?"

"Nothing's wrong," said Steve.
"You won the contest. That was some great trick riding. How did you all fit on one board?"

"We make a great team," said Fred.

"A great surf team!" said Velma.

Scooby barked. "Scooby-Dooby-Doo!"

The End